The Berenstain Bears®
and the
HICCUP CURE

Stan & Jan Berenstain

A GOLDEN BOOK • NEW YORK
Western Publishing Company, Inc., Racine, Wisconsin 53404

What lovely fruit,
Mama Bear.
May I have
this yellow pear?

Yes, Papa Bear.
But remember the past.
You know what happens
when you eat too fast.

GOBBLE-GOBBLE!
CHUFF-CHUFF!

DRIBBLE-DRIBBLE!
GLUFF-GLUFF!

Eat slowly, dear.
You know I worry
when you eat
in such a hurry.

What happened, Mama,
in the past
when Papa Bear
ate too fast?

Hiccups happened
in the past
when your papa
ate too fast.

Hiccups? Nonsense!
Calm your fears.
I have not
had those in years!

Do not worry.
I happen to know
hiccups are something
you outgrow.

So relax, my dears.
I think you'll find
I've left my hiccups
far behind!

I hate to say
I told you so,
but they are *not*
a thing you outgrow.

When you gobble
like a pig,
you get hiccups.
You get them *big*!

HIC

HIC

HIC

HIC

HIC

HIC

I must admit
that I was wrong.
I've got hiccups.
I've got them strong.

HIC

HIC

HIC

Don't just stand there!

One thing is sure.

I need some help!

I need a cure!

Take a deep breath
then don't breathe again
until I've counted
from one to ten.

HIC

HIC

HIC

10

Hold my breath?
Are you sure
that really is
a hiccup cure?

HIC

HIC

HIC

You want a cure—
Well, I know how.
Just hold your breath
starting . . . NOW!

11

Mama! Mama!
What shall we do?
Papa Bear
is turning blue!

All right, dear.
Start breathing, please.

Phew! That cure is worse
than the disease!
But, golly gee!
It's great to be
hiccup-free!

Thank you very much,
my sweet.
I'll be more careful
how I eat.

Don't look now,
Mama Bear.
But Papa's hiccups
are still there!

HIC

HIC

HIC

HIC

Help me, please.
This hic, hic, hic
is making me
feel sick, sick, sick!

15

I just remembered
another cure.
Sips of water!
That's the cure!

HIC HIC

HIC

Please, my dear.
Are you sure?

I'll *bet* on it!
I'm very sure
it's the no-fail
hiccup cure!

Drink slowly, Papa!
Keep on sipping!
Careful, now.
The water's dripping.

That one worked!
What a relief!
I'm cured! I'm cured
of hiccup grief!

HIC! HIC! HIC!

HIC!

HIC!

HIC!

HIC!

My dear, it seems
you've lost your bet.
I still have hiccups.
Now I'm also soaking wet.

Look! Papa Bear
is turning green!

It's the worst case of hiccups
I've ever seen.
Brother, go get your mask
from Halloween.

Why a mask?
May I ask?

We're going to cure
Papa Bear
by giving him
a great big scare.

Now this is what
you have to do:
jump out at him
and holler BOO!

Brother Bear,
I have to ask.
Why are you wearing
that stupid mask?

HIC HIC

I put it on
to scare you, Pop,
and make those
awful hiccups stop!

You can't scare me,
Brother Bear.
I'm big and strong!
I'm Papa Bear!

We must cure him.
We'll do it yet.
And a scare is still
our best bet.

Yes, we must!
Yes, we ought!
But how to scare him?
Wait! I have a thought!

These hiccups—hic!—
won't leave me alone!
Uh-oh! Why are you
picking up the phone?

I'm calling five, five, five,
one, one, three, two.
It's the doctor's number.
When I get through,
I'll make a hiccup
appointment for you.

A hiccup appointment!
But what, my dear,
can a doctor do?

I would say,
like as not,
you'll get some sort
of hiccup shot.

29

Hiccup shot?
Golly Gee!
Hiccup shot?
Woe is me!

Come on, Papa!
We're on our way!
Doctor will see you
right away!

Wait a minute!
Dear, please wait.
I have some news
that's really great!
We need not see
the doctor today.
Those nasty hiccups
have gone away!

The next time
Papa eats too fast,
as he has done
in the past,
I'll know exactly
what to do.
Dial five, five, five,
one, one, three, two!